Clever Ali

NANCY FARMER

Illustrated by GAIL DE MARCKEN

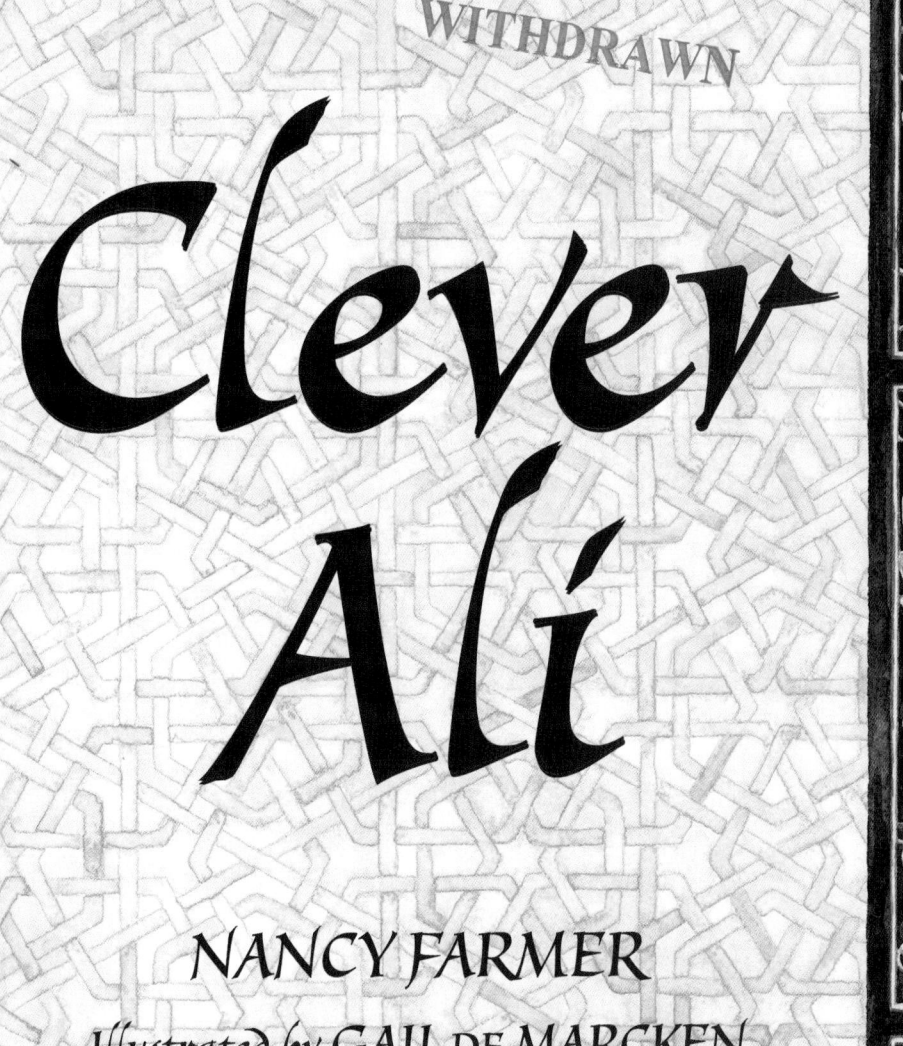

ORCHARD BOOKS

An Imprint of Scholastic Inc./New York

From **In Praise of Books**

A book is a garden you can hold in your hand,

An orchard you can take on your lap.

A book is a companion who sleeps

Only when you are asleep,

And speaks only when

you wish him to.

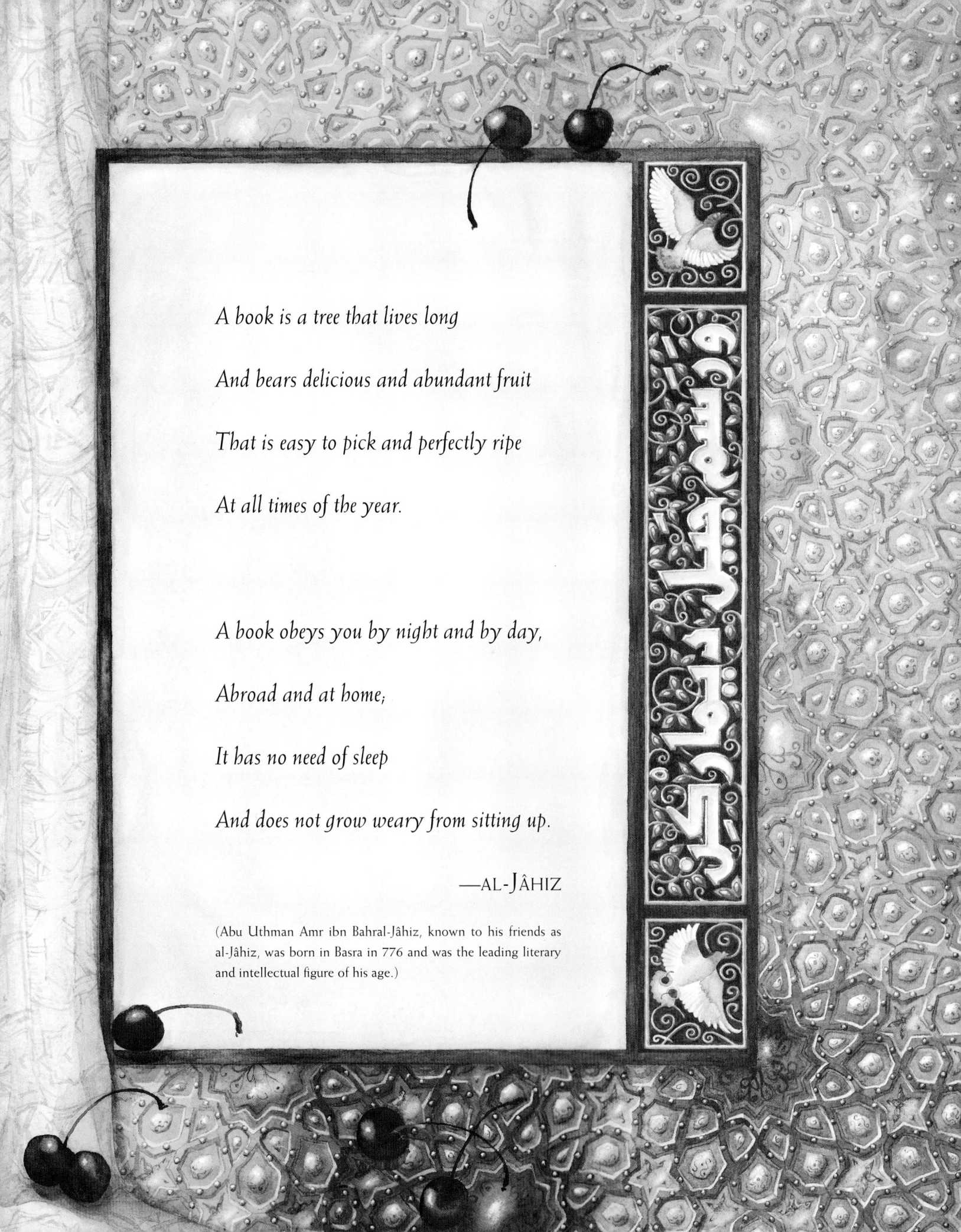

A book is a tree that lives long

And bears delicious and abundant fruit

That is easy to pick and perfectly ripe

At all times of the year.

A book obeys you by night and by day,

Abroad and at home;

It has no need of sleep

And does not grow weary from sitting up.

—AL-JÂHIZ

(Abu Uthman Amr ibn Bahral-Jâhiz, known to his friends as al-Jâhiz, was born in Basra in 776 and was the leading literary and intellectual figure of his age.)

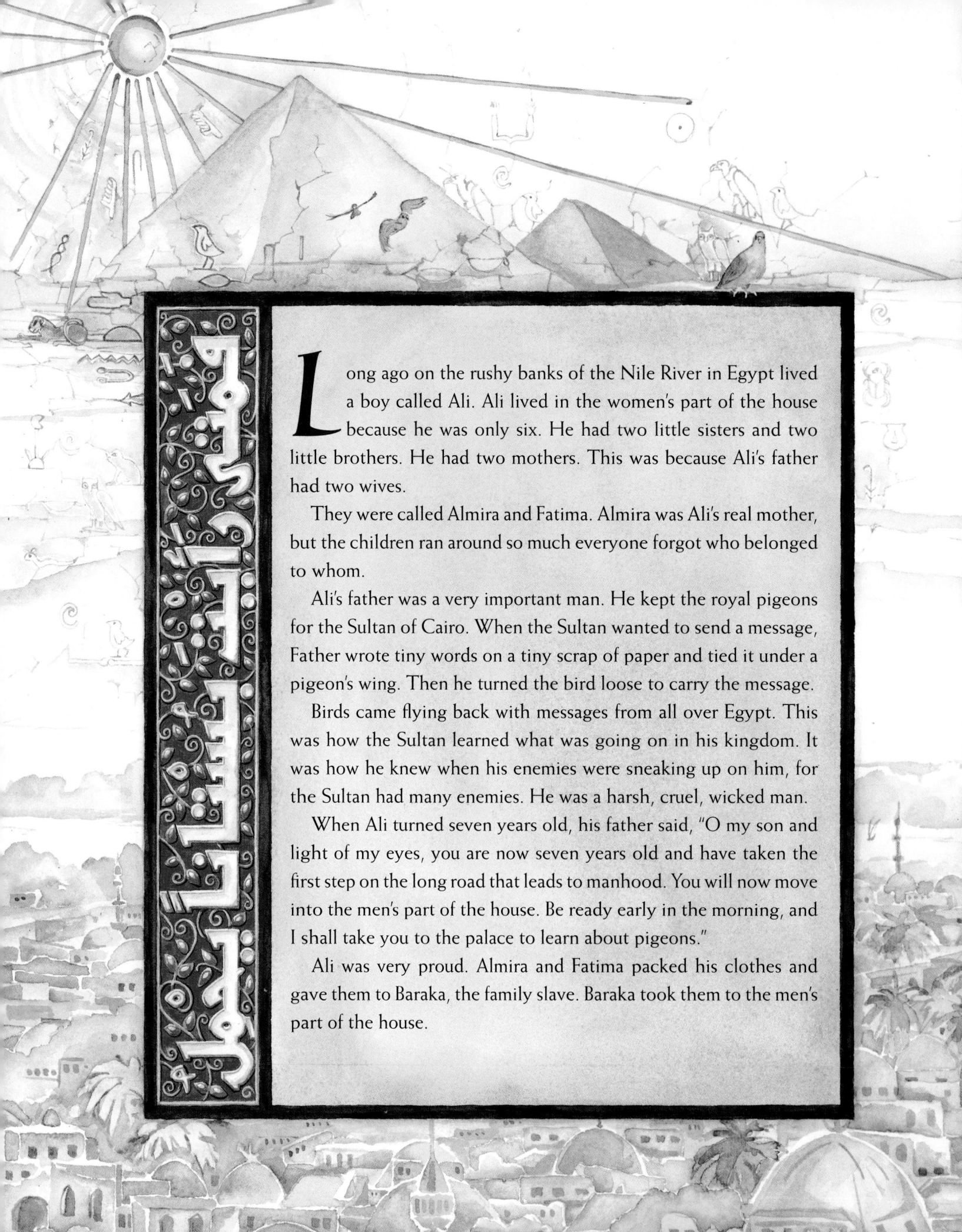

Long ago on the rushy banks of the Nile River in Egypt lived a boy called Ali. Ali lived in the women's part of the house because he was only six. He had two little sisters and two little brothers. He had two mothers. This was because Ali's father had two wives.

They were called Almira and Fatima. Almira was Ali's real mother, but the children ran around so much everyone forgot who belonged to whom.

Ali's father was a very important man. He kept the royal pigeons for the Sultan of Cairo. When the Sultan wanted to send a message, Father wrote tiny words on a tiny scrap of paper and tied it under a pigeon's wing. Then he turned the bird loose to carry the message.

Birds came flying back with messages from all over Egypt. This was how the Sultan learned what was going on in his kingdom. It was how he knew when his enemies were sneaking up on him, for the Sultan had many enemies. He was a harsh, cruel, wicked man.

When Ali turned seven years old, his father said, "O my son and light of my eyes, you are now seven years old and have taken the first step on the long road that leads to manhood. You will now move into the men's part of the house. Be ready early in the morning, and I shall take you to the palace to learn about pigeons."

Ali was very proud. Almira and Fatima packed his clothes and gave them to Baraka, the family slave. Baraka took them to the men's part of the house.

Baraka was very large and stood at the front door with a big, curved sword to keep out thieves. He came from a land to the south where the sun was big and where men wrestled crocodiles for sport.

Ali had a bedroom all to himself in the men's part of the house. He was afraid of being alone, but he said nothing. He didn't want anyone to think he was a baby.

Early in the morning, when it was just light enough to see the difference between a white thread and a black thread, Ali was ready. Almira and Fatima and his two little sisters and two little brothers stood at the door and cried, "Woe, woe, woe! When shall we ever see you again?"

"Don't be silly," said Father. "We'll be back by dinnertime." Then Father and Ali set out for the palace through the cool, dark streets of Cairo. The city was just waking up. Men led donkeys from their stables. Women hurried to the market to buy fish from the rushy banks of the Nile River. The palace guards did exercises to keep their muscles strong.

The palace grounds were so enormous that Ali was afraid. *I'll never find my way around here*, he thought. But he said nothing because he didn't want anyone to think he was a baby.

Finally, after many twists and turns, they came to the pigeon loft. It was a large building with three rooms. The first room was for the women pigeons. The second was for the men pigeons. In the third lived the married pigeons and their babies. Outside was a courtyard with a beautiful little fountain made of blue stone.

"You must never let pigeons fly at night or in the rain or when they are hungry," Father said. "Most of all and most importantly, you must never, never feed them too much. If you feed them too much, they will become spoiled and selfish."

The sun was just then climbing over the walls that surrounded the palace. It shone on the little fountain, making the water sparkle. Ali thought the splashing fountain and the cooing pigeons were the nicest sounds he'd ever heard.

"When a message comes in, the Sultan must be told at once," said Father. "If he's sleeping, someone has to wake him up."

"Doesn't he get angry?" said Ali.

"Yes," said Father. "He gets very angry. But he gets even angrier if he isn't woken up. He has many enemies and must know when they are creeping up on him. The Sultan has to be woken up slowly and carefully. His slaves play music and whisper compliments into his ear. One of them stands by his bed with a steaming hot cup of coffee. When the Sultan is truly awake, I read him the message. It has to be done exactly right."

"And if it isn't?" said Ali, holding his breath.

"Then, O my son and light of my eyes, the first person the Sultan sees is thrown straight into his deep, dark oubliette."

It was a strange word. Ali had never heard it before. It came in three parts like the three rooms in the pigeon loft. The first part, *Oooooo*, sounded like a wind in the palm trees on a cold winter night. The second part, *Bleeeee*, was like the cry of a lost gull in the hot, dry desert. The third part, *Et!*, snapped like the jaws of a jackal on a fat little hen.

"What," said Ali, "is an oubliette?"

"An oubliette, O my son and light of my eyes, is a deep, dark hole. The Sultan learned about oubliettes from the Frankish barbarians who live to the north and who never bathe. The Frankish king keeps them for his enemies. He throws them inside and they fall down, down, down until they go *kerplop*."

"*Kerplop?*" Ali said faintly.

"*Kerplop*," said Father firmly. "The minute the Sultan heard about oubliettes, he wanted one of his very own. He has, as you know, many enemies. His soldiers dug a hole in the throne room. They dug for forty days and forty nights and on the forty-first day—"

Father stopped talking as servants came into the pigeon loft. They carried baskets of broad beans. Everyone scurried around, opening cages and sweeping them out. Fresh water was put into bowls. Mustard leaves were tied to the perches for the pigeons to nibble. Father peered into the nests. When he found a new baby, he wrote its name in a book and complimented its parents.

Ali worked as hard as anyone. At the end of the day he was so tired he fell asleep. Father took him home on a donkey.

Ali woke up when they reached home. Baraka was standing in front of the door with his arms folded and the big, curved sword in his belt. Almira and Fatima and Ali's little sisters and brothers were waiting inside. "Oh, joy! Oh, joy! You have returned to us!" they cried.

"Of course we have," said Father. "We said we'd be back by dinnertime."

Ali and Father sat on the carpet. Almira poured water over their hands, and Fatima dried them with soft, white towels. Then Baraka carried in a long, low table for dinner. They had spiced lentils and rice cooked with sheep's feet for flavor. They had quails stuffed with almonds and raisins. For dessert they had wonderful little cakes sticky with honey.

When Ali was only six, he had to wait for dinner until Father was finished. Now he was seven and had taken the first step on the long road that leads to manhood. He ate at the same time as Father. Baraka, Almira, Fatima, and his little sisters and brothers had to wait, but they didn't mind (much). They were used to it.

"What happened on the forty-first day?" asked Ali.

"I will tell you tomorrow," said Father.

Early in the morning, when it was just light enough to see the difference between a white thread and a black thread, Ali and Father set out for the palace. Almira and Fatima and his two little sisters and two little brothers stood by the door and cried, "Woe, woe, woe! When shall we ever see you again?"

"Don't be silly," said Father. "We'll be back by dinnertime."

They walked through the dim, blue streets of Cairo. Sleepy donkeys complained loudly as their masters woke them up. Fishermen hurried by with nets full of silver fish from the rushy banks of the Nile River.

"I didn't want to tell you about the forty-first day until we were away from the house," said Father. "I didn't want to upset Almira and Fatima. They worry so much about the palace. They'd *really* worry if they knew what went on there.

"On the forty-first day," said Father, "the soldiers broke through to an enormous cave under the ground. It was as big as a whole city. The walls were made of rubies and the floor was made of gold. It was lit by red fires, and in the middle was a huge and horrible demon."

"Oh, Father!" cried Ali.

"The soldiers could only see the top of his head. He was sitting in an armchair and drinking a steaming hot cup of lava. The soldiers climbed back out of that hole as fast as mice fleeing from a cat. Their captain threw himself in front of the Sultan and cried, 'O great and terrible master, we have dug into the home of a demon. Please let us fill in the hole before he notices.'

"The Sultan stroked his bushy, black beard. 'Demon, you say?'

"'Yes, O great and terrible master,' said the captain. 'He's as big as a hundred elephants. He has horrible black horns and long scaly arms and huge purple claws.'

"'Is his ceiling a long way or a short way from the top of his head?' said the Sultan, still stroking his bushy, black beard.

"'A long way, master,' said the captain.

"'And is the light in the cave bright or dim?'

"'It is dim, my lord,' said the captain. ·

"'Then he'll never be able to see the hole in the ceiling!' cried the Sultan. 'I have the only oubliette in the whole world with a demon at the bottom. The Frankish king who lives to the north and who never bathes will be green with envy!'

"From that day on," said Father, "the Sultan has thrown people he doesn't like into the oubliette. But the worst thing of all—" Father stopped and looked carefully around the street. There was only a woman shaking out bedding from a high window. Ali waited, hardly daring to breathe.

Father bent down until he was able to whisper into Ali's ear. "The worst thing of all is this: When someone is thrown inside, he falls down, down, down *and doesn't go kerplop!*"

"He doesn't?" gasped Ali.

"There's no sound at all. Nothing."

And that, Ali thought, was truly awful. It was bad, of course, to fall down, down, down and go *kerplop*, but far worse to do nothing. You wouldn't know what was waiting for you until you got to the bottom. You might fall into the demon's jaws to be munched up like a stick of celery. Ali felt sick just thinking about it.

"And now," said Father, straightening up, "it's time to take care of the pigeons."

After a few weeks, Father gave Ali a young bird to train. "Listen carefully, O my son and light of my eyes. This isn't a pet. He must learn to work hard and carry messages for the Sultan. Most of all and most importantly, you must never, never feed him too much. If you feed him too much, he will become spoiled and selfish."

"I promise," said Ali.

Ali named the pigeon Othman. He trained Othman to come when he whistled. He taught him to fly back to the pigeon loft from anywhere in the palace. Every time Othman did as he was told, he was given a handful of food.

From the very beginning Othman was greedy. He ate as many broad beans as he could get, but what he really liked were nuts and dates and honey cakes. Ali saved up his desserts from home. He brought them to Othman, who gobbled up every crumb.

One day it was time to teach Othman a new task. He had learned to find his way from anywhere in the palace. Now he had to find his way from somewhere else. Baraka came to work with Father and Ali. He packed Othman's cage and put Ali in front of him on a fine, white horse.

They rode through the crowded streets of Cairo until they came to the quiet gardens on the rushy banks of the Nile River. There, Baraka unpacked a picnic lunch. He and Ali watched the river slide by as they munched on white cheese and olives. Baraka told Ali stories about the land to the south where the sun was big and where men wrestled crocodiles for sport.

All the while, Othman paced back and forth in his cage. He hadn't been fed that morning. He grumbled and grumbled, watching Baraka and Ali eat. "Can't I give him something?" asked Ali.

"No, indeed," said Baraka. "The hungrier he is, the faster he'll fly back to the pigeon loft."

So Ali finished his lunch with one of Almira and Fatima's wonderful little cakes sticky with honey. He licked his fingers. All the while, Othman grumbled and paced back and forth in his cage.

Finally, Baraka nodded, and Ali opened the cage. Othman waddled out. "That's the fattest pigeon I ever saw," said Baraka. "Are you sure you haven't fed him too much? A bird who eats too much will become spoiled and selfish."

"I hope not," said Ali, thinking of all the desserts he had saved for Othman.

Othman waddled around, eyeing the spot where Baraka and Ali had eaten lunch. There wasn't a crumb left. He grumbled to himself.

"Pick him up and throw him into the air," said Baraka.

Ali picked up the bird and smoothed his feathers. "You can do it," he whispered. He climbed onto a rock and threw Othman into the air. The bird gave a startled squawk and opened his wings. Up, up, up he soared. He had to do this in order to see the palace. Ali held his breath. "There he goes!" he cried.

Baraka and Ali rode through the crowded streets of Cairo. They went around donkeys loaded with pots. They went around fishermen loaded with nets. They almost knocked over a fruit stand. But Baraka was a very good horseman and didn't hit anything.

All the while Othman flew overhead. He flew slowly because he was a very fat pigeon. Many times he landed on the tops of buildings to rest. "He shouldn't do that," said Baraka.

Ali didn't say anything. He silently promised to put Othman on a diet. But the bird didn't rest for long. He took off again, going up, up, up to catch sight of the palace.

Finally, he got there. But instead of going to the pigeon loft, he went in the opposite direction. Ali slid off the horse and raced through the courtyards to catch him.

"Othman! Othman!" he called. He whistled. He waved his arms. The bird paid no attention.

The pigeon dived through a door, and Ali ran after him. The door was guarded by huge guards with big, curved swords in their belts. They yelled and chased after Ali. They called their friends, and soon there were fifty men yelling and running through the halls.

Ali didn't dare stop. He had to catch Othman before he got into trouble. He ran through one last door and skidded to a halt.

It was a big, round room with beautiful pink walls and green curtains. A hundred lamps hung from the ceiling. In the middle of the floor was a huge hole. It was the Sultan's oubliette.

On the other side, sitting on a golden throne, was the Sultan.

He was being served a bowl of cherries by a slave girl. Othman swooped down and grabbed a cherry. The slave girl screamed and dropped the bowl. Cherries rolled in all directions. The fifty guards rushed through the door and trod on them. They slipped and slithered and teetered and tottered. They bellowed and bawled and grabbed on to one another until they skidded to a halt right in front of the oubliette.

Othman landed on the floor and began eating.

The room was very quiet for a moment. The only sound was *peck-peck . . . peck-peck* as Othman worked his way across the squashed cherries. Ali could only stare in horror.

The Sultan was a tall, thin man with a cruel mouth. He had a long, thin nose. His face was chalk white and his beard was as black as midnight. Two little spots of red danced in his coal-black eyes.

"Bring me that pigeon," said the Sultan.

Instantly, the guards untangled themselves and pounced on Othman.

"Show me his foot," said the Sultan.

Now Ali was really frightened. Every one of his father's pigeons was marked on the foot with a little crescent. It showed that the bird belonged to the palace and wasn't wild. When the Sultan saw the crescent, he would have Father thrown into the oubliette. Father would fall down, down, down until he landed in the demon's jaws to be munched up like a stick of celery.

"Bring me the Keeper of Pigeons," said the Sultan.

The guards rushed out and soon they returned with Father. He looked perfectly calm, as though he'd been invited for a cup of mint tea. He didn't act frightened at all. Ali was very proud of him.

Father bowed deeply and said, "O great and terrible master, what is your command?"

"I was enjoying a bowl of cherries," said the Sultan. "They were brought to me by swift ship from the snowy mountains of Syria. There are no more cherries anywhere in the land of Egypt—and your pigeon has knocked them all over the floor."

"I deeply regret this young bird's foolishness," said Father calmly. "I will bring you oranges and melons from the market. I will bring you grapes bursting with sugar and plump figs coated with honey."

"No! No! No!" roared the Sultan. "Only cherries will do! I want cherries! I want them now!" He hurled his turban to the floor and stamped on it. He hurled himself to the floor and rolled around, kicking and screaming.

He looked exactly like Ali's little brothers when they threw tantrums. Any minute now, the Sultan was going to hold his breath until he got what he wanted.

But the Sultan got up instead and pointed at Father. "Cast this man into my oubliette!" he shouted.

"No!" cried Ali, running forward. "It's my fault! I trained him and I spoiled him." He threw himself on the floor before the Sultan. He felt very small and very, very alone.

"My son is only a small child," said Father.

"Silence!" yelled the Sultan. He sat on his throne, stroking his bushy, black beard. Ali looked up into the two little spots of red dancing in his coal-black eyes.

The Sultan smiled. It was a cruel smile, and it didn't make Ali feel any better. "I will give you one chance," the Sultan told Father. "If this boy can bring me a bowl of six hundred cherries in three days, I will forgive you. If not, down the oubliette you go."

"O great and terrible master, that's impossible," said Father. "Cherries only come by swift ship from the snowy mountains of Syria. It takes two weeks."

"That's your problem," the Sultan said. "Until the sun sets in three days, you will stay in my dungeon. Run, boy, run! Find my cherries and save your father's life!"

Ali didn't waste a second. He ran all the way back to the pigeon house. Othman, who flew out the window when the Sultan had his tantrum, had got there first. He was stuffing himself full of broad beans.

"You horrible bird!" said Ali. "I hope you choke."

But Othman didn't choke. He kept on eating.

Ali found Baraka and told him what had happened. "We must go to every market in Cairo to buy cherries," said Ali.

"There aren't any," said Baraka. "Cherries only come by swift ship from the snowy mountains of Syria. It takes two weeks."

"We have to do something!" cried Ali. "If we don't find them, the Sultan will throw Father into the oubliette. He'll be munched up by the demon like a stick of celery!"

"I think we should go home," said Baraka. "Almira and Fatima are as full of good sense as a pomegranate is full of seeds. They may have an idea."

Ali dreaded going home. He knew Almira and Fatima were going to weep and wail. To his great surprise, they sent the small children out to play and set about making mint tea.

"I thought you'd be upset," said Ali.

"We worry before something happens," said Almira. "It's silly to worry after it happens."

Soon they were all sitting around the long, low table with cups of mint tea. "Now it's time to make a plan," said Almira.

"I think we should buy grapes and paint them red," said Fatima.

"The paint is poison," said Baraka.

"Who cares?" Fatima said.

"The Sultan will never be fooled," said Almira. "He's as rotten as a three-day-old egg in the hot sun, but he's not stupid."

"We could make cherries out of clay and bake them in the oven," Fatima said.

"The Sultan would break his teeth on them and throw us all into the oubliette," said Baraka.

"He's as nasty as a rat in a bucket full of dead earthworms," said Almira. "I hope he *does* break his teeth."

While they were talking, Ali began to have an idea. It was such a clever, wonderful, amazing idea, he could hardly believe he thought of it by himself. It *could* work. It *would* work. It was too clever, wonderful, and amazing not to.

He told Almira, Fatima, and Baraka. They all sat back in admiration. "What a smart boy you are," said Almira.

"I always thought he was," said Fatima.

"We'd better go to the palace at once and get started," said Baraka.

He and Ali rode through the crowded streets of Cairo on the white horse. They raced to the pigeon loft. Baraka wrote the message in tiny letters on a scrap of paper. He wrote it because Ali had only just learned to write and wasn't very good at it. Then they tied the message under the wing of a pigeon.

They sent nine more messages, each one exactly the same. This was in case some of the birds got lost or were eaten by hawks.

Then Baraka and Ali waited . . . and waited . . . and waited. For three days they waited in the pigeon loft. They were afraid to leave for a minute in case they missed something. On the afternoon of the third day, when the shadows were growing longer, Ali heard a fluttering and flapping in the air.

A great cloud of pigeons landed in the courtyard next to the fountain. They cooed and stretched their legs. They dipped their beaks into the fountain. They were very thirsty from their long trip over the desert.

"Hurrah!" cried Ali. For he had sent a message to the cherry farmers in the snowy mountains of Syria. And they had sent back three hundred pigeons with silk bags tied to their legs. In each bag was a cherry.

It may take two weeks for ships to sail from the snowy mountains of Syria, but it takes far less time to fly!

"We did it!" shouted Ali, dancing around. Baraka got a brass bowl, and Ali untied the silk bags and counted out the cherries. There were exactly six hundred of them.

The shadows were getting longer and longer. They had to get to the Sultan before the sun set. Baraka lifted the bowl and Ali walked ahead to open the doors. Suddenly, there was a flutter of wings. Othman swooped down and grabbed a single cherry from the top.

"Stop!" yelled Ali, but it was too late. The greedy pigeon landed on a high perch and gobbled up the cherry.

"We don't have time to wait," Baraka said.

Ali snatched a grape from his lunch basket and buried it at the bottom of the bowl.

"Come on!" said Baraka. They hurried through the halls and courtyards until they came to the Sultan's throne room. The Sultan was sitting on his throne, watching a monkey wrestle a bear cub.

The last red rays of the sun shone on the walls.

"How on earth did you get those cherries?" said the Sultan. He sounded disappointed.

Ali told him.

"Well, well. I see you are as clever as your father. But are there really six hundred cherries in that bowl?" said the Sultan.

"Yes," said Ali with a horrible, sinking feeling.

"We shall see." The Sultan ordered another bowl. He began counting the cherries into it. The sun went down. The slaves came in to light the lamps. The Sultan kept counting. "Three hundred and fifty-one . . . three hundred and fifty-two . . ." until he got to the bottom of the bowl, when he said, "Five hundred and ninety-nine . . . Aha! The last one's not a cherry! It's a grape! You tried to trick me!"

Ali thought he would cry. He had been so close.

"And now," said the Sultan in a soft voice, "because you tried to trick me, I'm going to throw *you* into the oubliette."

The guards held Baraka so he wouldn't fight. They grabbed Ali and tossed him into the hole. Before Ali could say *help!* he was already falling down, down, down into the inky darkness of the oubliette.

I hope it's quick, he thought as he fell. *I wonder if demons munch up their food or if they swallow it whole.*

In the next second Ali fell out the bottom of the hole into an enormous cave. It was as big as a whole city. The walls were made of rubies, the floor was made of gold, and it was lit by red fires. Ali fell *whump!* onto something very soft. He sat up, coughing from the dust. He was sitting in an enormous armchair.

"So that's why nobody heard *kerplop* when the Sultan threw people into the oubliette," said Ali. "*Whump* simply doesn't travel very far."

Not far away he saw a crowd of very unhappy people. They were sitting on the ground and eating what looked like tree roots. Beyond them was a demon as big as a hundred elephants. He had horrible black horns and long scaly arms and huge purple claws.

He was stirring a pot of boiling lava. Emeralds and sapphires bobbed around inside like vegetables. The demon licked his lips with a long, snaky, black tongue.

He turned around and saw Ali. "Oh no!" he said in a deep, rumbly voice. "Not another human! And this one's a baby!" He put down the spoon he was using to stir the lava. "This is really too much," said the demon to himself. "It isn't enough I have to put up with earthquakes. I keep having this rain of humans from the ceiling. It's annoying. It's unfair. What have I done to deserve it?"

He bent down and looked at Ali with a round, yellow eye. Ali smelled his breath. It was worse than three-day-old eggs in the hot sun and buckets full of dead earthworms.

"I suppose you won't say any more than the rest of them." The demon sighed. "You're only a baby."

"I am *not* a baby," said Ali, standing as tall as he could in the soft easy chair. "I'm seven years old and have taken the first step on the long road that leads to manhood."

"Well, well. It talks," said the demon. "Maybe you can tell me why I'm bothered day and night by a rain of humans. Why do you come here? You don't have a good time. All I can feed you is tree roots."

So Ali told him about the Sultan and his oubliette. He told him about Father and the pigeons and how the Sultan got angry when he only got five hundred and ninety-nine cherries.

"He sounds like a bad man," said the demon.

"He is," Ali said.

"Do you mean these humans don't *want* to be here?" said the demon.

"They hate it. They'd leave in a second if you'd let them."

"They should have told me." The demon smiled at the crowd of people. His teeth were orange and as sharp as a cobra's fangs. The people moaned and clung to one another.

"How do they get in?" asked the demon. Ali pointed to a tiny black dot in the ceiling far away. "As much as I enjoy talking to you," said the demon, "I suppose you want to go home."

"Very much," said Ali.

"Then you can take these others with you." The demon stretched up his arm. It grew longer and longer. It disappeared up the hole. "Climb out. I'll wait," he said.

"Come on!" shouted Ali to the crowd of unhappy people. He started climbing the demon's long, scaly arm. The scales made it easy to get a foothold. Ali went up a long way. He waved and shouted, "Come on! Do you want to stay here forever?"

Then everyone ran to the arm and started climbing. Up and up and up they went. Now and then they had to sit on skin bumps to rest, but the demon was very patient.

Finally, Ali came to the top and jumped out into the throne room. The guards were cowering against the walls. The demon's arm snaked out of the hole like a monster tree root. His purple claws were curled around the Sultan.

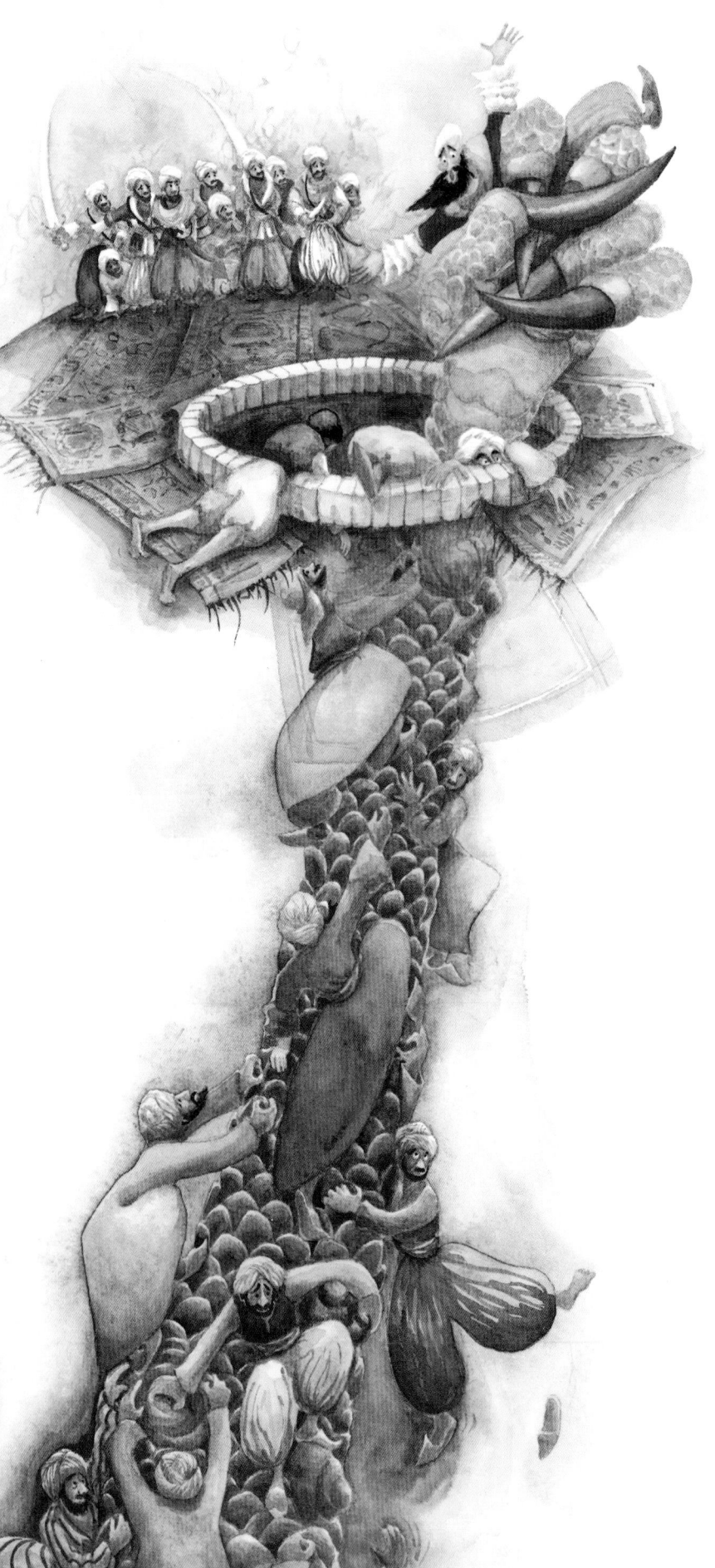

One by one, all the people climbed out. When the last one was free, the arm snaked back down the hole. Last of all came the hand with the Sultan. "Nooooooo," wailed the Sultan on the way down. Ali listened carefully. He didn't hear *kerplop*. He didn't hear *whump*. And—he was glad about this—he didn't hear *munch, munch, munch*, either.

The Egyptians were so happy, they made Ali's father Sultan instead. They made Ali the crown prince. Father freed Baraka and made him the Keeper of Pigeons. The demon plugged up the hole in his ceiling with rubies, emeralds, sapphires, and diamonds. They spilled out into the throne room. Almira and Fatima turned some of them into necklaces.

As for Othman, he was no use as a message carrier. Ali's little sisters kept him as a pet. They fed him honey cakes until he was too fat to fly, but Othman didn't care. He was very happy.

And so was everyone else.

Author's Note

Homing pigeons have been used to carry messages for more than two thousand years. The ancient Greeks used them to carry news of victory at the Olympic Games, and Roman generals kept Rome informed of their movements with the birds. But probably no one had a better message system than the medieval rulers of Egypt.

There were almost two thousand birds in the pigeon loft of Cairo and hundreds more at relay stations along the main travel routes. A pigeon flew only one stage of a long trip. When he arrived, hungry and tired, at a relay station, his message was given to another pigeon who flew it on to the next stop.

Pigeons flew only one way: toward home. The Egyptians believed that pigeons were devoted to their mates. The male bird was taken away by donkey while the female remained in her nest. When he was given a message to carry, they believed he would fly home eagerly because his wife was waiting for him.

The letter was fastened under his wing, to keep rain from spoiling it. Nowadays, with better ink and paper, messages are tied to a bird's leg.

Records of a pigeon's genealogy and medical history were kept as carefully as racehorse owners keep records of their horses today. A really good pigeon could cost as much as seven hundred golden dinars.

Clever Ali is based on a true story. The Egyptian ruler Al-Azeez in about A.D. 1190 had a craving for fresh cherries. A message was sent by pigeon to Syria. Six hundred pigeons were sent back with silk bags tied to their legs. Three days after saying he wanted cherries, Al-Azeez was served a bowl with twelve hundred of them. If he ate all of them, he probably got a stomachache.

Artist's Note

Since representational art is rare in the Arab-Muslim world, I have used the fantastic designs of their various cultures to give an Arabic flavor to the pictures. The patterns behind the text blocks were copied from mosaics, woodwork, plaster, and marble from Cairo's mosques and Islamic antiquities. For example, the pattern surrounding the translation of al-Jâhiz's words is a wildly colored repetition of the pattern of a bronze door in the madrassa-mosque of Sultan Hasan (1356–63).

Calligraphy is a vital art form in the Arab world. There is a great love of the written word, so it seemed fitting to use calligraphy as an integral part of the border designs. In each border, I have painted, in Arabic, the adaptation of al-Jâhiz's "In Praise of Books," the poem at the opening of this book.

While the countries of North Africa and the Middle East speak different vernaculars, they all read and write classical Arabic, the language of the Koran. It is read and written from right to left. Many beautiful styles of forming letters have been crafted through the centuries. The style I used is a modern version of Kufic, one of the earliest forms to evolve and which is known from Spain to Iraq. The endpapers give the English sounds of the Arabic consonants.

To Bailey Ives Coppola

–N.F.

For my Nina

–G.D.M.

Special thanks to Edward Jajko, Curator Emeritus of the Middle East Collection, Hoover Institution, Stanford University, for his long and careful study of ancient Arabic texts to get the language and translation exactly right; to Hisham Khalek, Director of the Arabic Language and Culture Program, University of Minnesota, for meticulously supervising the Kufic script of the Arabic language as it appears in Gail de Marcken's art; and to Tanner Bina for posing as Ali.

Grateful acknowledgment is made for permission to use an adaptation of the translation of "In Praise of Books," found in *Night and Horses and the Desert: An Anthology of Classical Arabic Literature*, edited by Robert Irwin (Woodstock, New York: The Overlook Press, 1999, pp. 84–100).

Library of Congress Control Number: 2005027133
ISBN 0-439-37014-0
10 9 8 7 6 5 4 3 2 1   06 07 08 09 10
Printed in Singapore   46
First edition, October 2006
The artwork is rendered in watercolor.
The text type was set in 13-point Weiss Medium.
Book design by Kristina Albertson

BIBLIOGRAPHY
Glubb, John Bagot. *Soldiers of Fortune, The Story of the Mamlukes*. New York: Stein and Day, 1973.
Zim, Herbert Spencer. *Homing Pigeons*. New York: William Morrow & Co., 1949.

This book belongs to:

LIGHT

JANE BRESKIN ZALBEN

DUTTON CHILDREN'S BOOKS

DUTTON CHILDREN'S BOOKS
A division of Penguin Young Readers Group

Published by the Penguin Group
Penguin Group (USA) Inc., 375 Hudson Street, New York, New York 10014, U.S.A.
Penguin Group (Canada), 90 Eglinton Avenue East, Suite 700, Toronto, Ontario, Canada M4P 2Y3
(a division of Pearson Penguin Canada Inc.) • Penguin Books Ltd, 80 Strand, London WC2R 0RL, England
Penguin Ireland, 25 St Stephen's Green, Dublin 2, Ireland (a division of Penguin Books Ltd)
Penguin Group (Australia), 250 Camberwell Road, Camberwell, Victoria 3124, Australia
(a division of Pearson Australia Group Pty Ltd) • Penguin Books India Pvt Ltd, 11 Community Centre,
Panchsheel Park, New Delhi - 110 017, India • Penguin Group (NZ), 67 Apollo Drive, Rosedale,
North Shore 0745, Auckland, New Zealand (a division of Pearson New Zealand Ltd)
Penguin Books (South Africa) (Pty) Ltd, 24 Sturdee Avenue, Rosebank, Johannesburg 2196, South Africa
Penguin Books Ltd, Registered Offices: 80 Strand, London WC2R 0RL, England

LIBRARY OF CONGRESS CATALOGING-IN-PUBLICATION DATA

Zalben, Jane Breskin.
Light / by Jane Breskin Zalben. — 1st ed.
p. cm.
"Inspired by a sixteenth-century midrash (a legend based on a biblical text) . . .
by Rabbi Isaac Luria of Safed (1534–1572)."
Summary: A retelling of the midrash about the creation of light.
ISBN 978-0-525-47827-0 (alk. paper)
[1. Creation—Folklore. 2. Jews—Folklore. 3. Folklore.] I. Title.
PZ8.1.Z2825Li 2007
398.2—dc22 [E] 2006102948

Published in the United States by Dutton Children's Books,
a division of Penguin Young Readers Group
345 Hudson Street, New York, New York 10014
www.penguin.com/youngreaders

Designed by Elizabeth Frances

Manufactured in China
First Edition

1 3 5 7 9 10 8 6 4 2

Author's Note

This myth I wrote was inspired by a sixteenth-century *midrash* (a legend based on a biblical text). It was written by Rabbi Isaac Luria of Safed (1534–1572), who founded the Kabbalah—mystical teachings in Judaism. In his poetry, he saw the story of creation this way: When the world originated, God planned to put sparks of light into everything. The holy light was stored in vessels, but it was so strong, the vessels broke into millions of pieces. People were made to find these shards of light, bring them together, and restore the shattered vessels, thereby "repairing the world" (*tikkun olam* in Hebrew).

Many world religions have practices of "healing the world" and "renewing the earth." Can human beings fix a broken world? If only we could see sparks of light in every part of creation. An insect wing. A blade of grass. A streaked pink-and-blue sky. And most of all in each other. Then the world might be a more peaceful place. Sometimes we feel helpless, hopeless. But with love, caring, and acts of kindness, everyone has the power to repair one small piece of a broken world—and make it whole.

Jane Breskin Zalben

In the beginning there was emptiness, like a blank canvas.

Then, in a swirl of motion,

the Creator made the world.

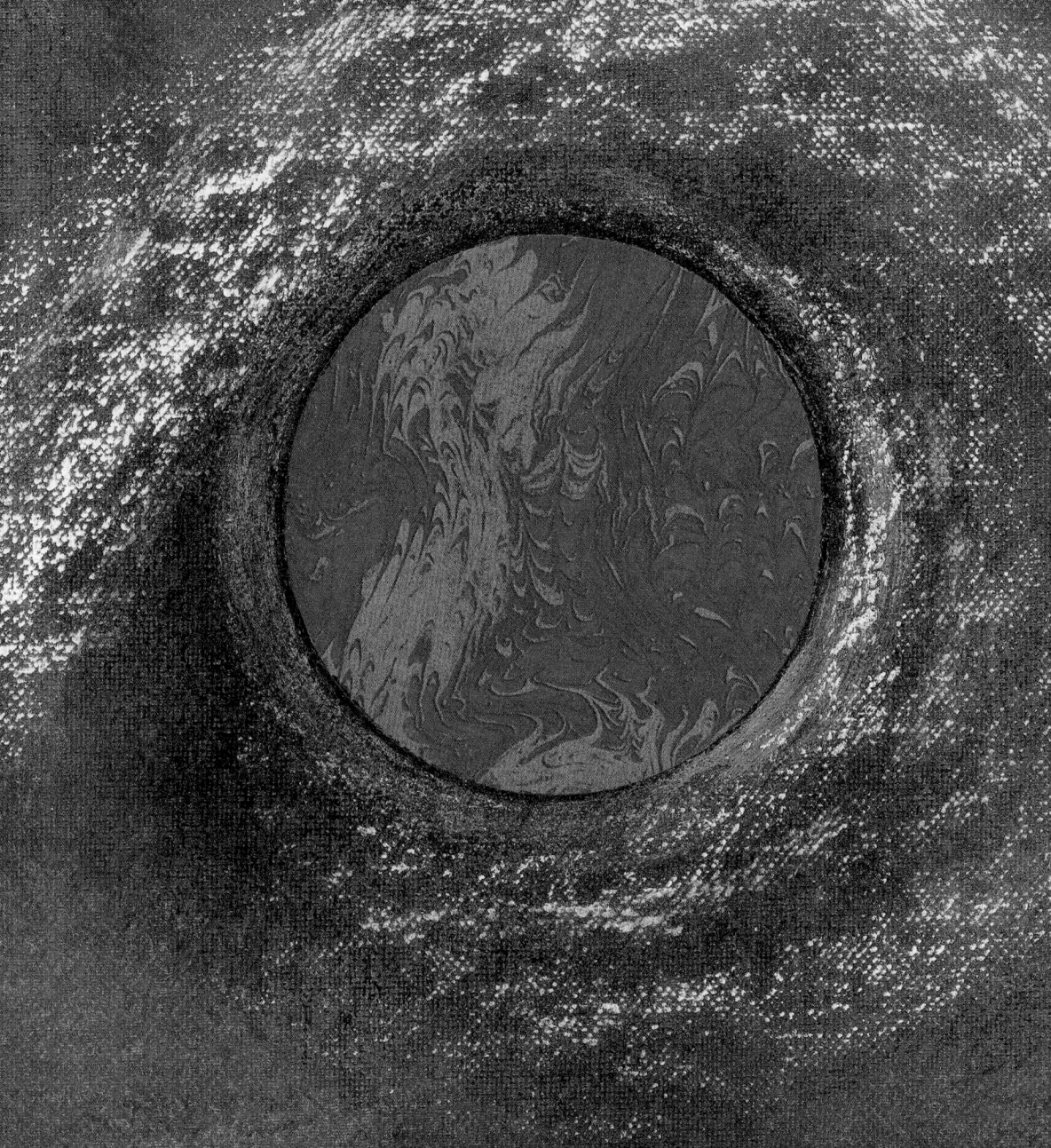

The sun, the moon, and
the stars were born.

**Still waters became
rivers and oceans.**

**Land became deep valleys
and high mountains,**

blossoming with lush plants,
trees, and fruit.

**Animals of all shapes,
sizes, and colors
appeared in the water,
on the land,
and in the clear blue sky.**

As a finishing touch,
the Creator wanted to paint everything
with a special kind of light
so the world would shine with goodness.
The light was so powerful,
it had to be stored away in a huge jar.

**But when the Creator
started to open the jar,
it shook violently,
tipped over,
cracked,
and shattered.
Sparks of light flew out.**

The Creator couldn't find
the missing pieces alone.
Who could help?

Birds?
Frogs?
Beasts?

Then the Creator had an idea.

People were made
to find the shards of light
and bring them together again.
Only then would the world be
complete and perfect.

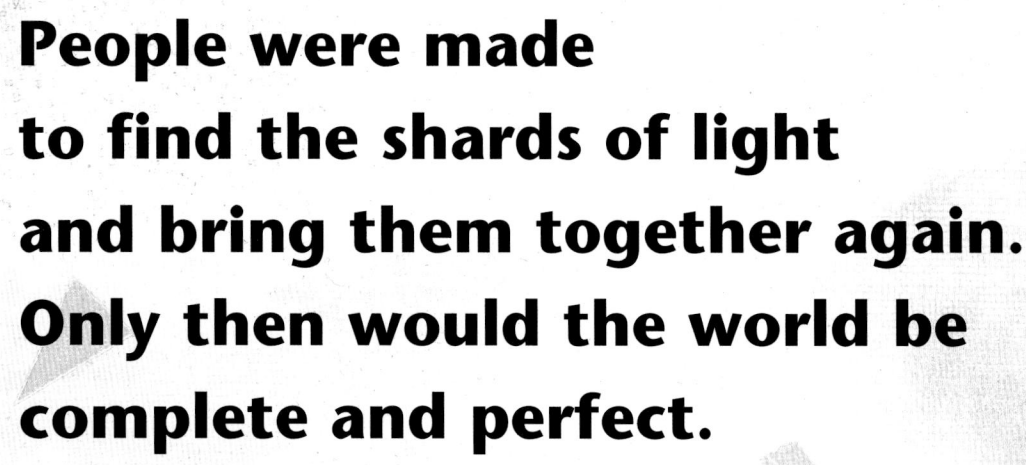

People searched far and wide.
They spied pieces
sparkling on blades of grass,
shimmering on sea kale,
and glistening on insect wings.

They saw the light
in animals' loving eyes.

**They discovered it in each other
and, sometimes, in themselves.**

**Whenever people found the light,
they felt contentment,
joy,
and peace.**

**When they shared it with one another,
there was no more hate,
hunger,
fear,
or war.**

Many shards are still to be discovered.
The world is incomplete
and far from perfect.

As long as people are searching
for the pieces of light,
finding them,

and putting them back together,
then there is hope that

the world will be one.

Art Notes

In my mind, *Light* is the final picture book in my "trilogy" that deals with peace. The journey began after September 11, 2001, when I decided that I could no longer work in the way I had been working for so many years. I started experimenting with different materials, papers, fabrics, styles, and methods. In doing so, this picture book emerged. But in a strange way, it is a "coming home" to where I began—painting on canvas. Once again I decided to do this book differently from all my others. To take another journey.

The exciting part was exploring technique after the text was done. How would I actually depict shards of light? With light itself. And so I used acrylic and oil paints; liquid acrylics; pastels; colored pencils; oil crayons (saved from when I was five years old and still intact!); gel polymer medium mixed with sand, dirt, leaves, grass, table salt, sea salt; linseed oil; water; turpentine; baking powder; Comet, Windex, and Clorox sprays; quinoa seeds; kasha grains; seaweed; flower petals; berries; and vines, often drying the art in the open air during various seasons—the book took well over a year to complete. I both added dimensions on and rubbed layers off to create serendipitous effects, using a knife, brushes, a burnisher, dental tools, cloths of various textures, paper towels, and sponges—both natural and mass-produced. The creative challenge was the *not* knowing where it would take me, which in a way is the book. If you leave yourself open, with an open heart, maybe you can give yourself a tiny piece of joy, happiness, and light in a very complex world.